I Don't Want to Comb My Hair!

Licensed by The Illuminated Film Company
Based on the LITTLE PRINCESS animation series © The Illuminated Film Company 2008
Made under licence by Andersen Press Ltd., London
'I Don't Want to Comb My Hair!' episode written by Cas Willing.
Producer Iain Harvey. Director Edward Foster.
© The Illuminated Film Company/Tony Ross 2008
Design and layout © Andersen Press Ltd, 2008.
Printed and bound in China by C&C Offset Printing.
10 9 8 7 6 5 4 3 2 1
British Library Cataloguing in Publication Data available.

ISBN: 978 1 84270 764 7 (Trade edition)
ISBN: 978 1 84939 692 9 (Riverside Books edition)

I Don't Want to Comb My Hair!

Tony Ross

Andersen Press · London

"Come back here!" cried the Maid. The Little Princess was
supposed to be having her hair combed.
"No!" The Little Princess grabbed the comb and made
a dash out of her bedroom and down the castle stairs.

By the time the Maid caught up with her, the comb had
mysteriously disappeared.
"I haven't got it," said the Little Princess, trying to look innocent.

It was time to tell the Little Princess's mum and dad.

"Another one!" said the King.

The Maid nodded. "That's five combs she's hidden this week!"

The Little Princess hid behind the King's armchair. Her hair was in a tangle, but combing it really hurt.

"Come out, Princess," sighed the Queen.

"Oh dear," said the Queen. "Maybe I'll take you to the hairdresser."

"No!" squealed the Little Princess.

"Do you want me to do it?" offered the King.

"I want to do it myself!"

The King, Queen and the Maid took a moment to think about this idea.

"You can be in charge of combing," agreed the Queen.

"But you **have** to do it!"

"I'm in charge of combing," grinned the Little Princess.
She marched outside and found her pram. She poked in rabbit
holes, rooted through vegetable patches and climbed up trees,
fetching all the brushes and combs she'd hidden.

"Look what's happened to this fish!" cried the Admiral,
when he spotted her near the pond.
The Little Princess giggled. "That's another one of my combs!"

Up in her bedroom, the Little Princess got started.
"I'll do everyone else first," she decided. "Then me, 'cos I'm
in charge of combing."
Some of her dollies needed to be combed very hard.

"Combing is hard work," puffed the
Little Princess. "I'm getting muscles."
She gave her doll's hair one last strong tug.

Per-lop!

Dolly's head had been combed off her body!

"Puss!" beamed the Princess, waving her comb in readiness. "You're next!"

"Miaoooww!" Puss screeched with horror, then tore out of the bedroom.

The Little Princess looked over to
Scruff and smiled. "Your turn!"

Scruff barked with delight, stretching flat so the
Little Princess could tickle his back.

The Little Princess scampered downstairs. Combing hair was fun.

"Must you?" asked the Prime Minister.

"I'm in charge of combing," nodded the Little Princess. "By order
of the Queen."

She carefully rearranged his three strands of hair, then set
off for her next job.

By the time she had finished with the Chef, he was speechless.

"They look very pretty," announced the Little Princess, admiring her handiwork.

By the afternoon, the Little Princess had nearly finished.
She'd de-tangled the General's hair, while he'd detangled his bearskin hat.

Next she'd made a beautiful daisy chain for the Gardener's shiny head.

Now she was working on the Admiral.
"Careful!" he chuckled. "This is my best beard."
"All done!" cried the Little Princess. "But I can't
find Puss anywhere."

"Princess!" called the Maid. "Dinnertime!"

"Better go," sighed the Little Princess. She would have to find Puss later.

In the royal bathroom, the Little Princess clambered onto the stool to wash her hands.

"AAaahhhhhhhHHHHH!!"

The Little Princess looking at her from the mirror was a frightening sight. Her hair was a mass of knotty tangles.

The Little Princess dashed out of the bathroom.
Upstairs she grabbed the biggest comb she could
find and started emergency de-tangling.

"Ow, ow, owww!"

The comb was stuck fast. She tried
another one, but that got stuck too!

"Dinnertime!" called the Maid from downstairs.
"Oh no!" the Little Princess gasped. "Now someone
else will do it. Maybe even the hairdresser!"

"Sweetheart?" asked the Queen, when the Little Princess came down for dinner.

The Princess adjusted her headscarf proudly. "I want to look just like you."

The King raised his eyebrows at the Queen. Something funny was going on.

At bedtime, the Little Princess looked even stranger.
"Bit cold tonight," she explained, when her dad
brought a glass of water.
"OK, poppet," frowned the King.

"Messy hair is not comfy," groaned the Little Princess the next morning. "I need help."

The Little Princess forlornly made her way downstairs. She found the Maid in the laundry, still wearing the bunches she'd put in the day before.

"That is horrible!" gasped the Maid.
"The worst rat's nest I have ever
seen." The Little Princess gulped.
Could rats be living in her hair?
Suddenly a mouse ran along the
castle window ledge and looked
right at her.

"AAAAHHHHHHHHH!!!"

The Little Princess burst into the castle sitting room.

"Cut it off!" cried the Little Princess. "The rats are coming!"

The King was puzzled. "A bald princess?"

"Cut it, cut it!"

"We can't cut hair, sweetheart," explained the Queen.

The Little Princess realised there was only one thing for it.
"Then take me to the hairdresser right now. Pleasssssse!"

"Come along, sweetheart,"
said the Queen. "We'll soon
have you sorted."
The whole castle came out to
wave off the Little Princess.
Everyone was relieved that
she was not in charge of
combing any more.

The trip to the hairdresser was a great success.

"I've got a new comb," beamed the Little Princess.

She quickly scooped Puss into her arms. "It's just right…

…for grooming cats!"

KT-434-072

To Ben, my pants-tastic illustrator ~ CF

For Ruth, with all my love ~ BC

SIMON AND SCHUSTER
First published in Great Britain in 2010 by Simon and Schuster UK Ltd
1st Floor, 222 Gray's Inn Road, London WC1X 8HB
A CBS COMPANY

A CIP catalogue record for this book is available from
the British Library upon request

ISBN: 978-1-4711-2326-9

Printed in China

5 7 9 10 8 6 4

Aliens Love Panta Claus

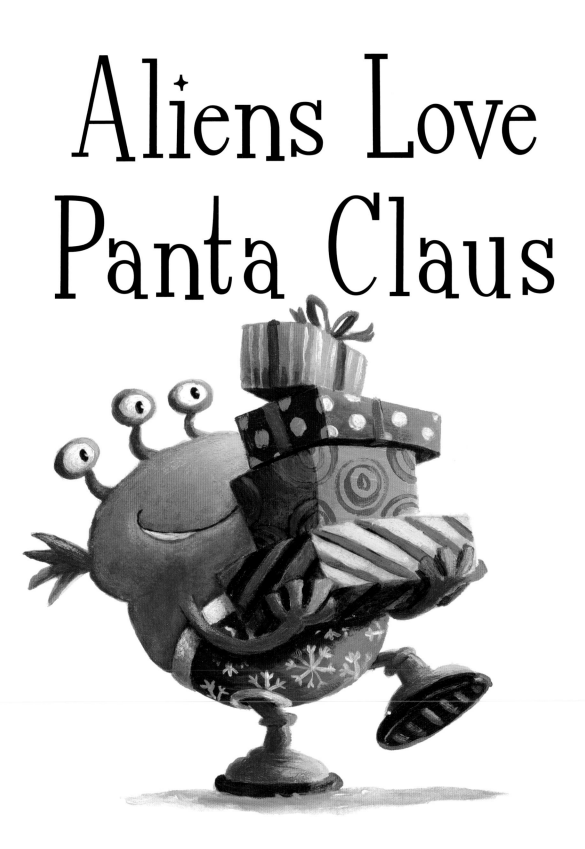

Claire Freedman & Ben Cort

SIMON AND SCHUSTER

London New York Sydney Toronto New Delhi

The aliens are excited,
As tomorrow's Christmas Day,
So instead of stealing underpants,
They're giving them away!

They jump into their spaceships – whee!
And whizz off to Lapland,
Full of the Christmas spirit,
To give Santa Claus a hand.

The aliens read the letters out,
From all the girls and boys,
And, just for fun, they add a pair,
Of pants in with their toys!

In Santa's busy workshop,
They cause lots of jolly snickers,
When dressing up the little elves,
In fancy, frilly knickers.

The reindeer wear their underpants,
Lit up all bright and glowing,
With neon pants to light the way,
It helps show where they're going!

Great! Santa's nearly ready,
But, shhh, when he turns his back,
The aliens swap a spotted pair,
Of bloomers for his sack!

"Ho-ho-ho!" laughs Santa,
But his smile turns to a frown,
He won't be going anywhere,
His sleigh has broken down!

It's aliens to the rescue,
With their spaceship for a sleigh,
So reindeer bells a-jingling,
Here comes Panta Claus — hooray!

They hover over rooftops,
And it really is fantastic,
How Santa shoots down chimneys,
On a rope of pants elastic!

The aliens follow Santa,
As he tiptoes to each bed,
They take down all the stockings,
And tie knickers up instead.

They decorate our Christmas trees,
With festive knicker cheer,
And leave out underpants that say,
"An alien woz 'ere!"

An alien woz 'ere!

Then, mission done, they fly back home,
To plan their next attack,
So hold on to your underpants,
The aliens **will** be back!